THE TWO-BY-TWO BAND

To ET and GR – read the original in Genesis 6 – D.F.

For Evie Norwood and an amazing future. Big love, Alibarts.

OXFORD
UNIVERSITY PRESS

Great Clarendon Street, Oxford OX2 6DP

Oxford University Press is a department of the University of Oxford.
It furthers the University's objective of excellence in research, scholarship,
and education by publishing worldwide in

Oxford New York

Auckland   Cape Town   Dar es Salaam   Hong Kong   Karachi
Kuala Lumpur   Madrid   Melbourne   Mexico City   Nairobi
New Delhi   Shanghai   Taipei   Toronto

With offices in

Argentina   Austria   Brazil   Chile   Czech Republic   France   Greece
Guatemala   Hungary   Italy   Japan   Poland   Portugal   Singapore
South Korea   Switzerland   Thailand   Turkey   Ukraine   Vietnam

Oxford is a registered trade mark of Oxford University Press
in the UK and in certain other countries

British Library Cataloguing in Publication Data available

ISBN: 978-0-19-272753-4 (Hardback)
ISBN: 978-0-19-272754-1 (Paperback)

10 9 8 7 6 5 4 3 2 1

Printed in China

Paper used in the production of this book is a natural, recyclable product
made from wood grown in sustainable forests. The manufacturing process
conforms to the environmental regulations of the country of origin

THE TWO-BY-TWO BAND

DAVID FLAVELL ♪ ALISON BARTLETT

OXFORD
UNIVERSITY PRESS

'When will it stop?' sighed Noah as he and the giraffes looked out at the rain.

'All I can hear is

PITTER-

PATTER, PITTER-

PATTER,

day and night.'

Mrs Noah was making supper.
'Turnips again, I'm afraid,' she said.
'We've been afloat for weeks
and the food won't last
much longer.'

'I know,' said Noah as he
served up the stew.
'But there's no sign of that
dove I sent out to find land.

The animals are getting grumpy
and looking at each other
hungrily, apart from the lions.

They're looking at me hungrily.'

'Music soothes the savage beast,' said Mrs Noah, 'so why not form a band?

I think the instruments are in the third cupboard from the left, on the second-to-bottom deck.'

'What a great idea!' said Noah,
and all the animals agreed.

They followed him down to
the cupboard and each pair
decided what to play.

The pangolins picked mandolins.

The marmosets snatched castanets.

The
baboons
chose
bassoons.

The great-crested
newts had bamboo
flutes.

The lions reached
for violins.

The three-toed **sloths** sat down at the **piano** together. Slowly.

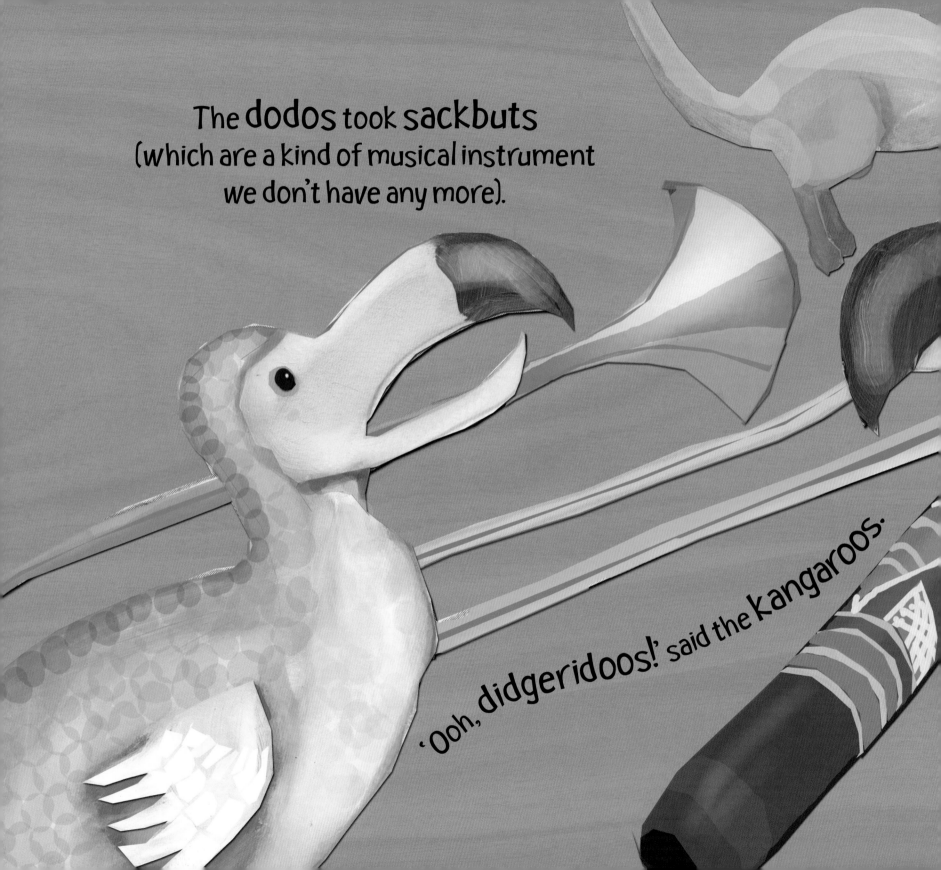

The **dodos** took **sackbuts**
(which are a kind of musical instrument
we don't have any more).

'Ooh, didgeridoos!' said the kangaroos.

The mice ran up the double bass.

And finally, the **elephants** were given what was left.

The **triangles.**

The Two-by-Two band
was ready to play.

'Let's make music!'
said Noah.

The baboons blew, the marmosets clicked,
the pangolins strummed, the lions bowed,
the sloths played a duet,
the great-crested newts tooted,
the dodos did whatever you do with a sackbut,
the kangaroos grooved,
the mice twanged,
and the elephants tapped their triangles.

It sounded dreadful!

'STOP!' shouted Noah.
Everybody stopped.
'What on earth is wrong?'

'You have to conduct an orchestra, dear,'
said Mrs Noah. 'What you need is a baton.'

'Where am I going to find one of those
out here?' asked Noah.

At that moment, Noah's dove flew back.
In her beak, she carried . . .

an olive branch.

'Thanks,' said Noah. 'I'll use this.'
Maestro Noah lifted up his new baton.

The elephants tapped their triangles,
the mice twanged,
the kangaroos grooved,
the dodos did whatever
you do with a sackbut,
the great-crested newts
tooted,

the sloths played a duet,
the lions bowed,
the pangolins strummed,
the marmosets clicked,
and the baboons blew.

And this time it sounded melodiously harmonious.
Marvellous music ebbed and flowed with
every sweep of Noah's baton.

'I wonder where the dove found this olive branch?'
he mused, as the band played on,
'because all the olive trees are under water.'

Noah and Mrs Noah and all the animals ran to the back of the ark and looked over the edge.

Sure enough, the floodwaters were beginning to go down, and they could see dry land.

The ark wobbled to a stop on a mountain top, and Noah heaved open the wooden doors to let the animals out into a happy new world.

As the Two-by-Two band disappeared
out of sight, Noah could still hear the
elephants tinkling their triangles.

'Just like the sound of raindrops!' he laughed.